MW01039831

Famous Illustrated
Speeches & Documents

The Gettysburg Address

Stuart A. Kallen

Illustrated by Terry Boles

Published by Abdo & Daughters, 4940 Viking Drive, Suite 622, Edina, Minnesota 55435.

Library bound edition distributed by Rockbottom Books, Pentagon Tower, P.O. Box 36036, Minneapolis, Minnesota 55435.

Printed in the United States.

Photo Credits Bettmann Archives, pages 9, 25
Archives photo, page 15

Illustrations by Terry Boles
Edited By: Julie Berg

Kallen, Stuart A., 1955—
    The Gettysburg Address / Stuart A. Kallen.
         p.   cm. -- (Famous Illustrated Speeches)
    Includes glossary page 40
    ISBN 1-56239-314-6
    1. Lincoln, Abraham, 1806-1865. Gettysburg address--Juvenile literature.
    [1. Lincoln, Abraham, 1809-1865. Gettysburg address.]
    I. Title II Series.
    E475.55.L76K35   1994
    973.7'349--dc20   94-7695
                              CIP
                              AC

PRESIDENT ABRAHAM LINCOLN

Abraham Lincoln was the 16th president of the United States. He was born February 12, 1809 in a log cabin in Hardin County, Kentucky. When Lincoln was nine, his family moved deeper into the wilds of southern Indiana. That same year his mother died.

By the time Lincoln was 17 years old, he stood six-feet four-inches tall and weighed over 200 pounds. When his father decided to move to Illinois, Lincoln helped him. He split logs for fences and planted crops. But Lincoln was more than a good farmer. He could read well and had a deep interest in history, government and the law.

When Lincoln was 25, he was elected to the Illinois General Assembly. He was a gifted speaker and often delighted crowds with speeches about education and democracy. In 1837, Lincoln became a lawyer. In 1846, Lincoln was elected to Congress, where he served one term.

During the following years, debates raged in the United States over the issue of slavery. Lincoln was strongly against it. In a series of debates, Lincoln became famous for fiery statements. He called for an end to slavery.

In 1860, Lincoln was elected president of the United States. Although he was pleased to be elected, Lincoln knew that the country was sliding into civil war. Lincoln believed that there would be no peace unless all people were free.

THE CIVIL WAR

The South had been using African-Americans as slaves to grow cotton and tobacco for 150 years. The people of the North wanted to stop this practice. The Southerners decided to break away and form their own nation. The Northerners did not approve. The Civil War then began in April 1861. The war tore America apart.

The battle of Gettysburg began by accident. In early summer 1863, the Confederate army invaded Pennsylvania, north of Washington, D.C., in search of food and clothing. The Union army trailed alongside, both sides waiting for the best chance to strike. On July 1, Confederate scouts, many by now barefoot, approached the town of Gettysburg to raid shops and a shoe factory. There they ran into Union horsemen.

There was some shooting. Then fiercer fighting. Soon the attacks doubled in size, then tripled. It would become the largest single land battle in history, involving 163,000 soldiers.

The first day, the Confederates seemed to be winning. On Day 2, the Union defense tightened and held firm. On Day 3, low on ammunition and other supplies, the Confederates turned around and retreated to Virginia.

The war would continue for nearly two years. But the Gettysburg battle swung the tide of victory to the North. The little Pennsylvania town became a huge outdoor hospital and burial ground. The Union army had lost about 23,000 men, the Confederates about 28,000 men — dead, wounded or missing.

A sacred resting place was needed, where the dead could be honored and remebered. Gettysburg would become a National Cemetery, and President Lincoln was asked to speak at the dedication on Nov. 19, 1863. Lincoln accepted.

INTRODUCTION TO THE ADDRESS

Lincoln entered the cemetery at the head of a parade. Dozens of Generals, Senators, and officials climbed onto the tiny stage with the president.

At 2 o'clock, a voice cried, "ladies and gentlemen, the President of the United States." Lincoln turned to the Secretary of State who sat next to him and said about his speech, "It is a failure. They won't like it."

Lincoln rose slowly to thundering applause. He paused. His eyes swept over the former battlefield where thousands of dead were buried.

Shouts of "Quiet please!" and "Down in front!" rose among the jostling crowd. A muffled din of voices rose from the outskirts. By the time people had quieted down, Lincoln was halfway through his very short speech.

In the days before electricity and microphones, politicians had to master the art of shouting words above a crowd. He spoke slowly and clearly. After a few sentences, his shrill voice took on a rhythmic, musical quality. He said:

Fourscore and seven years ago,

Lincoln often quoted from the Bible. In a speech given in 1838, he quoted Psalm 90, saying. "The days of our years are three score ten." (That's 70 years.) Later, the phrase, "Fourscore and seven years ago" would echo those Biblical words.

A "score" is twenty years. Four score is 4 X 20, or 80 years. "Four score and seven years ago" is 87 years ago. Lincoln was referring to the year 1776, when the Declaration of Independence was written and signed.

our fathers brought forth upon this continent a new nation,

Four days after the Gettysburg victory, Lincoln gave a short speech at a party on the White House lawn. In that speech, Lincoln used a few phrases that would later end up in the Gettysburg Address. He spoke of Washington, Adams, and the Founding Fathers.

Lincoln was speaking of the Founding Fathers of the United States such as Thomas Jefferson, Benjamin Franklin, John Adams, and George Washington.

conceived in liberty and dedicated to the proposition that all men are created equal.

People

The Founding Fathers did not really give everyone equal rights with the Declaration of Independence and the Constitution. African-American men could not vote until after the Civil War. Women of any race could not vote until 1920. Native Americans could not vote until 1924.

Lincoln was talking about the ideas that he felt the United States was founded on. They are written in the Declaration of Independence and the Constitution. These documents gave some U.S. citizens freedom and equal rights.

Now we are engaged in a great civil war,

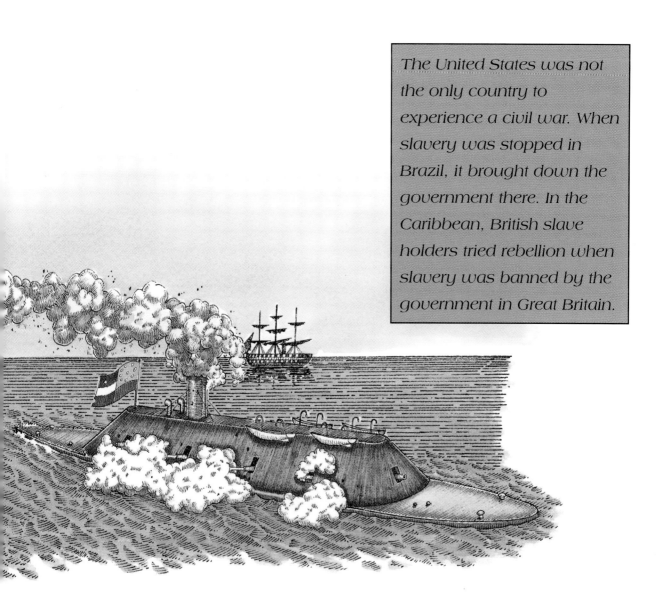

The United States was not the only country to experience a civil war. When slavery was stopped in Brazil, it brought down the government there. In the Caribbean, British slave holders tried rebellion when slavery was banned by the government in Great Britain.

The United States was divided into the North and the South, and the two sides were fighting. When any country breaks up and fights against itself, it is called a civil war.

testing whether that nation, or any nation so conceived and so
dedicated can long endure.

*Group portrait
of slaves before
their cabin,
1861.*

People in the North were not the only ones against slavery. Many groups fought it in the South. In one famous vote in Virginia, slavery was almost outlawed in 1832.

The Civil War was testing whether the United States — or any nation — dedicated to liberty and equal rights, could survive after half the states left to form their own country.

We are met on a great battle field of that war.

The land where Gettysburg National Cemetery was built was bought for $2,475.87.

The Gettysburg Address was given at the dedication of a cemetery. When Lincoln said that "We are met on... a battlefield..." he meant that the crowd was gathered where a great battle of the Civil War had been fought.

We have come to dedicate a portion of that field, as a final resting place for those who here gave their lives that that nation might live.

The Gettysburg Cemetery was divided into sections representing states. Soldiers were buried with others from their home state.

The cemetery was dedicated to the soldiers who died so that the nation "conceived in liberty" would survive.

It is altogether fitting and proper that we should do this. But, in a larger sense, we can not dedicate — we can not consecrate —we can not hallow — this ground.

Many had doubts about Lincoln speaking at the dedication. Some were afraid Lincoln would use the sad occasion for political purposes. And sometimes he talked for too long. Lincoln was asked to make a short speech. He only had two weeks to write what he was to say.

It is the right thing to do, but it is not possible for us to bless this ground because we were not part of the battle.

The brave men, living and dead, who struggled here, have consecrated it, far above our poor power to add or detract.

Lincoln was not the only speaker at Gettysburg on that day. Edward Everett was the key speaker. Everett was a former Senator, and a well-known poet.

The soldiers—living and dead—who fought for freedom at Gettysburg, blessed the ground better than anyone else could.

The world will little note, nor long remember, what we say here, but it can never forget what they did here.

Lincoln was saying that people would quickly forget the speech he was making but would remember the bravery of the soldiers forever.

It is for us the living, rather, to be dedicated here to the unfinished work which they who fought here have thus far so nobly advanced.

The Civil War raged for another 21 months after Lincoln spoke at Gettysburg. Many thousands more died to advance the cause of freedom.

The living must carry on the work of freedom and liberty that the fallen heroes had begun.

It is rather for us to be here dedicated to the great task remaining before us— that from these honored dead we take increased devotion to that cause for which they here gave the last full measure of devotion—

54th. MASSACHUSETTS VOLUNTEERS

Not every person in the North was glad to fight the Civil War. People with money could hire someone to fight for them. In New York City there were riots protesting the army draft. More than 1,000 people died in the riots.

If the living truly honor the dead, then they must continue the fight for freedom. The fallen soldiers made the ultimate sacrifice —death.

that we here highly resolve that these dead shall not have died
in vain—

The United States was made whole again on April 9, 1865, when Robert E. Lee and the Confederate Army surrendered. Slavery was officially abolished eight months later.

We vow that the soldiers will have died for a good reason.

that this nation, under God, shall have a new birth of freedom—

After the Civil War, slavery was ended and African-American men were given the right to vote.

The United States shall have a new burst of freedom.

and that government of the people, by the people, for the people, shall not perish from the earth.

Lincoln has been credited with writing the sentence, "of the people, by the people, and for the people." But at least 12 other writers have been credited with inventing the phrase. Lincoln could have gotten the words from an antislavery writer, Theodore Parker.

The government is chosen by everyone voting. It is run by the common people's wishes. And it is run for the common people's desires. It will survive the war and remain dedicated to those ideas.

AFTER THE SPEECH

And all of a sudden, it was over. Lincoln had spoken for only two minutes —271 words, 10 sentences. There was little applause. The crowd was stunned. They expected more from their president. At other times, Lincoln had been known to ramble on for hours. The band played a final tune, and the crowd broke up. As the people walked away, they began to turn Lincoln's words over in their minds. The speech began to take on special meaning to those who could hear it that afternoon.

Newspaper reporters ran to file their stories. The telegraph lines started clicking and clacking the president's address across the wires. By the next day, Lincoln's message would become part of America's history. The next day's newspaper editions called the speech "an immortal English classic."

In time, Lincoln's words became known as one of the finest speeches ever given. But it did not happen overnight. First, a war needed to be won. On April 9, 1865, the leader of the Confederate Army, Robert E. Lee surrendered in Virginia. The Civil War was over. Slavery would be outlawed and freed slaves given citizenship. The United States was made whole again.

Less than a week later, on April 15, President Abraham Lincoln was killed by an assassin's bullet.

The Gettysburg Address

Fourscore and seven years ago our fathers brought forth upon this continent a new nation, conceived in liberty and dedicated to the proposition that all men are created equal.

Now we are engaged in a great civil war, testing whether that nation or any nation so conceived and so dedicated can long endure. We are met on a great battle field of that war. We have come to dedicate a portion of that field as a final resting place for those who here gave their lives that that nation might live. It is altogether fitting and proper that we should do this.

But, in a larger sense, we cannot dedicate— we cannot consecrate— we can not hallow— this ground. The brave men, living and dead, who struggled here, have consecrated it, far above our poor power to add or detract. The world will very little note, nor long remember, what we say here, but it can never forget what they did here. It is for us the living, rather, to be dedicated here to the unfinished work which they who fought here have thus far so nobly advanced. It is rather for us to be here dedicated to the great task remaining before us— that from these honored dead we take increased devotion to that cause for which they gave the last full measure of devotion— that we here highly resolve that these dead shall not have died in vain— that this nation, under God, shall have a new birth of freedom— that government of the people, by the people, for the people, shall not perish from the earth.

GLOSSARY

Abolish - to end.

Conceive - to form an idea.

Confederate Army - the army of the Southern states. The Confederate Army was made up of soldiers from the states of Virginia, North Carolina, South Carolina, Mississippi, Alabama, Georgia, Florida, Louisiana, Texas, Arkansas, and Tennessee.

Consecrate - to make sacred.

Constitution - a system of rules and laws on which the United States was founded. The Constitution spells out how Congresspersons and Presidents are elected, and contains the Bill of Rights, which guarantees freedoms.

Endure - to continue to survive.

Engaged - joined together.

Founding Fathers - a term sometimes given to the men who began the American Revolution to gain independence from England. The Founding Fathers also signed the Declaration of Independence and wrote the Constitution. Some of the Founding Fathers were John Hancock, Benjamin Franklin, Thomas Jefferson, and George Washington.

Hallow - to make holy.

Martyr - a person who suffers or dies for a cause he or she believes in.

Proposition - plan or idea.

Slave - a person who is the property of another person and who is forced to work without pay.

Slavery - the practice of owning slaves.

Union Army - the army of the United States. The Union Army fought the Confederate army in the Civil War. The Union Army was made up of soldiers from Illinois, Delaware, West Virginia, Rhode Island, New Hampshire, Vermont, New Jersey, Wisconsin, Connecticut, Minnesota, Maryland, Maine, Michigan, New York, Pennsylvania, Massachusetts, Ohio, and Indiana.